Mimi's World
Book 2

Mimi's Treasure Trouble

LINDA DAVICK

Beach Lane Books

New York   London   Toronto   Sydney   New Delhi

BEACH LANE BOOKS • An imprint of Simon & Schuster Children's Publishing Division
1230 Avenue of the Americas, New York, New York 10020
This book is a work of fiction. Any references to historical events, real people,
or real places are used fictitiously. Other names, characters, places, and events are products
of the author's imagination, and any resemblance to actual events or places or persons,
living or dead, is entirely coincidental.
BEACH LANE BOOKS is a trademark of Simon & Schuster, Inc.
For information about special discounts for bulk purchases, please contact Simon & Schuster
Special Sales at 1-866-506-1949 or business@simonandschuster.com.
The Simon & Schuster Speakers Bureau can bring authors to your live event.
For more information or to book an event, contact the Simon & Schuster Speakers Bureau
at 1-866-248-3049 or visit our website at www.simonspeakers.com.
Book design by Lauren Rille
The text for this book was set in New Century Schoolbook.
The illustrations for this book were rendered digitally.
Manufactured in the United States of America
0819 FFG
First Edition • 10 9 8 7 6 5 4 3 2 1
Library of Congress Cataloging-in-Publication Data • Names: Davick, Linda, author, illustrator. •
Title: Mimi's treasure trouble / Linda Davick. • Description: First edition. | New York : Beach Lane
Books, 2019. | Series: Mimi's world ; 2 | Summary: Mimi and her fellow Gum Club members promise
to always stick together, but they soon discover it is hard to keep a group of six friends united
through thick and thin. • Identifiers: LCCN 2019000286 | ISBN 9781442458925 (hardback) |
ISBN 9781442458949 (eBook) • Subjects: | CYAC: Best friends—Fiction. | Friendship—Fiction.
| Clubs—Fiction. | BISAC: JUVENILE FICTION / Social Issues / Friendship. | JUVENILE
FICTION / Humorous Stories. | JUVENILE FICTION / Imagination & Play. • Classification: LCC
PZ7.D2815 Mi 2019 | DDC [Fic]—dc23 LC record available at https://lccn.loc.gov/2019000286

For Aggles

How It All

Happened

The Bubble Bursts

Loyal and True

The Gum Club

Mimi

That's me! My cat Marvin and I live on the top floor of the Periwinkle Tower. You can recognize me by my big yellow hat. I got it from Yoshi after the bad haircut he gave me. The purple convertible parked down by the drainpipe is mine. I can be out my window, down the drainpipe, and on the road in thirty seconds flat. Call me a dreamer, but it's my goal to be the first girl ever admitted to the Pueblo del Mar Reformatory.

Yoshi

is my smartest friend, but don't let him anywhere near your hair. He lives right below me and Marvin in apartment 3. He's *crazy* about books and carries one with him at all times. The only problem is that he can't read yet. But he *can* play the ukulele. Yoshi has a rich uncle who lives in Japan. We all call him Uncle Albert, and he sends us fantastic presents.

Tonya

lives right below Yoshi in apartment 2. She says she's had a hard life. She is very sensitive and likes quiet things like hairbrushes and mirrors. A sparkly tiara always holds her hair in place, though sometimes it pops off when she loses her temper. She enjoys supervising us.

Members

Boris

moved into the Periwinkle Tower last fall. He loves to eat. When you have lunch with him you have to be alert. If you look away for one second, he'll vacuum up your sandwich. His latest hobbies are making pudding and digging for dinosaur bones. Sometimes we play drums together after school.

Hunter

lives down the street from the tower. He's nuts about baseball. No one has ever seen his left hand because his baseball glove is permanently attached. He and Sofie can't have pets at home, so they take turns looking after Cheerio, our class rat.

P.S. We just found out that Hunter has a big brother who lives at the Reformatory! I can't wait to meet him.

Sofie

lives up the street. But her greatest wish is to live in the Periwinkle Tower. So we're digging a tunnel from her house to the tower to make her wish come true. Sofie has so many after-school activities that she often falls asleep standing up. When she dreams, if it's not about living in the Periwinkle Tower, it's about horses and ballet.

Springtime at the Periwinkle Tower

Hi, it's Mimi again! Reporting from the Periwinkle Tower, home of the Gum Club.

You've probably heard about the Periwinkle Tower. It's that tall apartment building in the middle of Pueblo del Mar. That's Spanish for "Village by the Sea."

1

Remember? We were in the news a few months ago when we won the Pueblo del Mar Holiday Decorating Contest. It was really Boris who won it for us with his gigantic stegosaurus.

It's funny. Last year I did everything I could to keep our group apart. That's because one of the Periwinkle residents drove me bonkers. I won't say who.

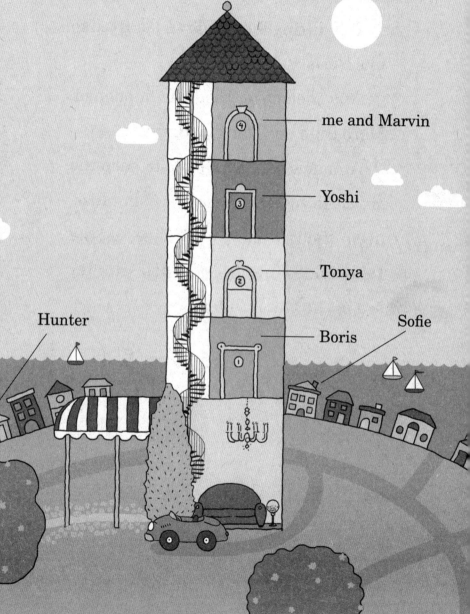

The Periwinkle Tower

me and Marvin

Yoshi

Tonya

Hunter

Boris

Sofie

But during the holidays, I started to like Boris.

And then something bad happened. More than one thing, actually.

And now it's all I can do to keep the six of us together. I say "six" because, even though they don't live in the Periwinkle Tower, Sofie and Hunter are in the Gum Club too.

The Gum Club Promise

Boris is the one who started the Gum Club. It happened when Uncle Albert gave him the gum ball machine at Christmas.

Every time we meet, we get in a huddle and shout out the Gum Club Promise:

"Six members loyal,
six members true.
We'll stick together,
whatever we do!"

Then we each crank a gum ball out
of Boris's machine, flop down on the
big red couch in the lobby, and talk
business.

Our club members are the best.

Yoshi runs upstairs to my door and gives the secret knock seven or eight times a day.

Tonya leaves pink perfumed notes for me. Even though her notes aren't always super friendly, it's not her fault. She has lots of allergies to deal with, and I'm sad to say that my cat, Marvin, is one of the worst.

Sofie loves visiting Marvin, even though Marvin prefers Tonya.

Hunter gives me all his baseball card doubles.

And Boris leaves chocolate-covered

raisins in my mailbox.

I love each and every one of the Gum Club members. And they love me!

So if you had told me that one day I was actually going to *break* the Gum Club Promise, I never would have believed you.

The Big Dig

Out my window I can see sailboats and a cruise ship on the ocean. In the backyard I can see a big hole. We're digging a tunnel, and every day it gets deeper and deeper.

The tunnel is our secret. The entrance is behind the tower, hidden

from view. It's the most exciting proj-
ect of our lives, even though it means
different things to each member of the
Gum Club.

The tunnel was Sofie's idea. It's her
dream to live in the Periwinkle Tower,

so we're aiming the tunnel toward her house. Once it's finished, she'll be able to sneak back and forth from her house to the tower without anyone seeing her. She'll be able to join us for midnight snacks.

She can spend the night on the big red couch in the lobby and be back home in time to get ready for school.

Hunter is crazy about forts. He thinks of the tunnel as one long underground fort.

Yoshi plays his ukulele down in the tunnel. He can sing as loud as he wants down there without bothering Tonya. Sometimes he finds rocks and bugs to look at under his microscope.

Boris is digging for dinosaur bones.

Tonya sees the tunnel as an opportunity to boss us around, which she loves doing. She calls it the Big Dig.

I'm not sure I should say out loud what the tunnel means to me. I don't want to jinx anything. But okay: maybe I can go ahead and write about it. It started with something Mr. Fogarty, the lighthouse keeper, said.

Field Trip

I'll explain. Last Wednesday morning Mr. Dayberry, our teacher, took our class on a field trip to the lighthouse.

That afternoon he said, "I'd like each of you to draw your favorite thing about the lighthouse. Then we'll bind the drawings together and make a book. We can mail it to Mr. Fogarty as a thank-you."

When we finished drawing, Mr. Dayberry said, "Yoshi? Show us your favorite thing."

Yoshi held up his drawing. "The spiral staircase. I counted 257 steps." Then he added, "There are only 70 steps in the Periwinkle Tower."

"So interesting! How about you, Tonya? What was your favorite thing?"

"All the mirrors around the light at the top."

"I think those were lenses, not mirrors," said Yoshi.

"They were mirrors. I could see my hair. I could see my tiara!"

"All right," said Mr. Dayberry. "Hunter?"

"This is the weather balloon that Mr. Fogarty launched. I love it that he is both our lighthouse keeper and our weatherman at the same time."

"You mean weather*person*," said Tonya.

"Boris, what did you like best?"

Boris held up a picture of a giant waffle. "My favorite thing was the waffle smell coming from the Lighthouse Café."

"The Lighthouse Café is not officially part of the lighthouse," Tonya pointed out.

"But the waffle smells from the café go inside the lighthouse, and Mr.

Fogarty gets to smell them every day!"

"But the café was not officially part of our field trip," said Tonya.

"But the waffle smells were in the lighthouse!"

Mr. Dayberry clapped his hands. "All right, let's move on. Sofie?"

"My favorite thing was the gift shop. So I drew a key chain. A mermaid key chain. I loved all the salt-and-pepper shakers that looked like little lighthouses. And the seashells, too."

"Why would you pay for seashells when you can find them on the beach?" asked Tonya.

"Did you see that big pink one?" asked Sofie. "You can't find those here. The sticker said 'China.'"

When I held up my drawing, Hunter laughed. "Mimi. You covered your page with yellow polka dots!"

"Those are gold doubloons. Millions of them. My favorite thing was when Mr. Fogarty told stories about all the

shipwrecks before the lighthouse was built. And how the shipwrecks got looted. That means there's probably buried treasure in Pueblo del Mar."

Now you can guess why *I'm* so excited about the Big Dig.

My Car Pool

Soon after Mr. Dayberry had collected our pictures, the bell rang. Sofie and I headed for my car. On Wednesdays she rides with me to the Periwinkle Tower to dig. Wednesday is the only day Sofie doesn't have ballet, horseback riding, piano, or Little Ninjas after school.

Mr. Fogarty had predicted blue skies, but it was sprinkling. I started to put the top up.

"I love riding in your convertible!" Sofie said. "Can we leave the top down?"

"Sure! Monday Tonya wanted the top up. And it was sunny!" Monday is Tonya's day to carpool.

"Tonya doesn't like the wind to blow her hair," said Sofie.

It's fun driving with my friends.

On Tuesdays, after he cleans

My Car Pool

Monday

Tuesday

Wednesday

Thursday

Friday

Cheerio's cage and brings him fresh water, I drop Hunter off at the ballpark. He hands me a baseball card as he jumps out. That's his way of saying thank you.

Thursdays Boris rides home with me. He talks about his new recipe ideas and asks for my opinion. When we get home, we play drums together until we hear Tonya come in.

On Fridays Yoshi rides home with me. He pulls his ukulele out of his backpack and all the way home he plays "Three Little Birds" and sings as loud as he can.

"Yoshi, you're a great singer," I yell over the wind. "Thank you!" he yells back.

"But I never hear you sing at home!"

"My singing bothers Tonya. Whenever I get to the part 'Every little thing gonna be all right,' she slams her window. The only places I can sing out loud are riding in your car and down in the tunnel."

Yoshi Calls a Meeting

It was Saturday. I hadn't seen Yoshi all day. I craned my neck out the window to see if I could spot him. The wind caught my hat and it sailed down across the yard.

I climbed out, grabbed the drainpipe, and slid down to chase it. That

hat is my most precious possession. It's become my official trademark, like Hunter's baseball glove or Tonya's tiara.

When I caught my hat, I climbed down and joined the others in the tunnel. Just as I picked up a shovel, we heard the Gum Club emergency whistle. We all know the emergency whistle means "urgent." We drop what we're doing, no matter what, and race toward the whistle fast as we can.

It was Yoshi! In the lobby. We ran inside and each of us cranked a gum ball out of Boris's gum ball machine. We brushed off our clothes and plopped down on the big red couch.

"I called this meeting of the Gum Club because I have some news," said Yoshi, looking around. "But does anyone know where Boris is?"

"Making pudding," said Tonya. "Pudding is his new hobby. I hear him making it all the time, and when I open my window weird pudding smells float up from his apartment."

Boris appeared with a bowl of pudding. He stood in front of the gum ball machine and cranked out one gum ball after another. Finally a sour apple gum ball bounced out. He popped it into his mouth and dropped all the others on top of his pudding.

Tonya rolled her eyes. "Boris, please don't tell me you're going to swallow those gum balls."

"No! I'm going to chew them along with the pudding."

I admire Boris. I know that someday he will be a great chef.

Yoshi's News

We stood up, made a huddle, and shouted out the Gum Club Promise.

"Six members loyal,
six members true.
We'll stick together,
whatever we do!"

Then we all flopped back down and looked at Yoshi. He didn't say anything at first.

"Yoshi, are you sad?" Sofie asked.

He nodded. "I have to go away this summer."

We all stopped chewing. Hunter dropped his baseball. "For the whole summer?" he asked. "Why?"

"Uncle Albert's coming. To take me to Boot Camp. In Colorado."

"Boot Camp?" Sofie's eyes got big and she kicked up a riding boot.

31

Yoshi's face turned red. He looked at the floor. "It's *Reading* Boot Camp. So I can learn to read."

My stomach did a flip-flop. "No!" I grabbed Yoshi's arm. "How will we star watch?" It was one of our favorite things to do in the summer. On clear nights Yoshi would bring his telescope outside, along with a blanket. We'd all lie on the blanket and look up at the sky.

"I'll leave my telescope here. You can use it." But we all knew it wouldn't be any fun without Yoshi pointing out the Big Dipper and the Little Bear.

"Who'll play the ukulele at my birth-day party?" asked Sofie.

"I'll make a playlist of my favorite songs for you," said Yoshi.

But we all knew nobody actually

got up and *danced* until Yoshi started playing his ukulele.

We're a gang of six. It's best when we're together. I know that someday in the future we might get separated. Some of us might have jobs, some of us might play professional baseball— and as for me, I plan to be living in the reformatory dormitory surrounded by stacks of gold doubloons. But until that time comes, we *need* each other.

Boris stirred his pudding. The gum balls made colored swirls. "I have an idea," he said. "Let's have a party to cheer us up."

"It's April," I said. "Whose birthday comes in April?"

Silence.

"Nobody's birthday comes in April?"

"Then let's have a party for Nobody!" said Boris.

We all smiled. "I'll make the invitations," I said.

Invitation with Dots

Back at home, I used my purple pen to make the invitations. Purple is my favorite color. And since dots make people laugh, I added zillions of them.

Soon as Yoshi found his invitation, he ran up and gave the secret knock.

"Will you read it to me?" he asked.

You are invited to a
Birthday Party for
NOBODY!
Tomorrow, Sunday, at 2:00,
on the BIG RED COUCH.
Wrap up something, ANYTHING,
so NOBODY will have PRESENTS to open.
P.S. Bring a snack if you'd like.

I read the invitation to Yoshi twice, so he'd remember. Suddenly I was determined to teach Yoshi to read.

Maybe then he wouldn't have to go to
Boot Camp. "The most important word
is "presents." I pointed to the word.
"P-R-E-S-E-N-T-S."

Nobody's Birthday Party

The next day at 2:00 the Gum Club met in the lobby. We each brought something we had wrapped. We lined up our presents on the coffee table along with our refreshments. We made a huddle and shouted out the Gum Club Promise.

Boris made pudding cupcakes.
Tonya carried in her teacup collection.
Sofie walked down the hill with a con-
tainer of chocolate ice cream. By the
time she opened it, it was melted and
ready to pour.

I picked all the Lucky Charms out
of a box of cereal and brought those.
Hunter threw down a bag of peanuts.
Yoshi brought a tiny piece of cheese for
Marvin.

Sofie sat back on the couch, starry-eyed. "I love drinking melted ice cream out of a teacup," she said. "I can't wait for the tunnel to be finished. I'll be able to have tea with you every night, and then I can fall asleep right here."

"Sofie, you go first," said Tonya. "Pick a present, any present."

Sofie chose a present wrapped in the comics page and tied with a blue shoe lace. She unwrapped it carefully.

"What *is* it?" she asked.

"It's a rock! I found it in the tunnel," said Yoshi.

"Oh, I love it!" said Sofie, holding it to her heart.

That's how nice Sofie is. The rest of us fell off the big red couch, we were laughing so hard.

Boris chose the package I had wrapped. "Chocolate-covered raisins!" he announced. "But the box has already been opened."

"That's strange!" I said. He bopped me on the head with the green pillow.

Yoshi's present was a pocket mirror. "I wonder who wrapped up *that* one," said Boris.

Yoshi glanced at Tonya. "It's great! I can use it to send SOS signals to ships at sea." He flipped the compact open and shut. The mirror gave three quick flashes, three slow flashes, and three quick flashes.

Tonya unwrapped her present. It was a stack of baseball cards tied with a ribbon.

"I'm afraid I can't use these," she said, handing the cards to Hunter. "But I love the ribbon. Watch this! I'll demonstrate how to make a pony-tail. May I borrow your pocket mirror, Yoshi?"

Hunter chose next. "What is *this*?" he asked, ripping the paper from his present.

"It's my favorite sock," said Boris. "It's argyle."

"But where's the other one?"

"I lost it."

We all cracked up. Some of Hunter's melted ice cream slopped out of his teacup onto the floor. Marvin cleaned it up.

I offered to refill Hunter's teacup, but he held up his baseball glove to block me. "I already have a stomach-ache from laughing so hard," he said.

The Pink Seashell

We were gasping for breath by the time I reached for the lumpy last present.

I couldn't believe my eyes. "It's the big pink shell! From the gift shop!"

"From China!" said Sofie. "I bought it with my allowance. Hold it up to your ear!"

"Shhhh!" I held the shell to my ear.

"What do you hear?" asked Yoshi.

I listened closely. "It says, *This is the happiest you'll ever be.*"

"Let me hear!" Boris popped the last pudding cupcake into his mouth. He grabbed the shell and held it to his ear. He closed his eyes. Then his eyes got really big. "You're right. It *does* say, *This is the happiest you'll ever be.*"

Everyone clamored for the shell. We passed it around.

"I can't understand a word it's saying," said Hunter. "I think it's speaking in Chinese."

We all laughed so hard we got the hiccups.

Yoshi picked up his ukulele and started strumming. We drank our ice cream and danced like crazy.

Then Yoshi played "Somewhere Over the Rainbow" and we all went home.

Sofie's Question

Every day after school that week I dug for treasure. On Wednesday Sofie could hardly wait to ride home with me to work on the tunnel. Boris showed up, and after baseball practice Hunter joined us. Tonya came out to supervise.

When it was almost dark, Yoshi

brought out his telescope. He asked us if we'd like to take a break to look at the moon.

Boris put his eye to the telescope and sang: "When the moon hits your eye like a big pizza pie . . ."

Then I peered through the telescope. The moon didn't hit *my* eye like

a big pizza pie. It looked like a giant gold doubloon hanging in the sky! I was so excited that I practically slid back down the ladder and continued digging harder than ever. I *knew* there was treasure down there. I could feel it.

"It looks like an enormous baseball!" I heard Hunter shout as he took a look. "Out of my way! I've got it!" Everyone laughed.

When I glanced up, Sofie was peering through the telescope. "Yoshi, I have a question for you."

"About the moon? Ask me anything!"

"No, it's not about the moon." She

took a deep breath. "You know I don't want you to go away this summer. But if you *have* to go, can I move into your apartment? Just for the summer?"

"I'd be happy for you to. But Mr. Bosco is repainting my apartment while I'm gone. And putting down carpet."

"*Sound*proof carpet," said Tonya.

"*Sound*proof carpet? Why?"

"I've asked Yoshi over and over not to play his music so loud. But he doesn't listen to me."

"I *do* listen, Tonya! It's just that . . . What am I supposed to do if I can't make music?"

"Read a book!" snapped Tonya.

Suddenly everyone got quiet. Yoshi looked down. If he had held the pink seashell from China to his ear at that moment, I know it would have said, *This is the most frustrated you'll ever be.*

"Oh, Yoshi!" said Tonya. "I meant to say, *look* at a book. A picture book maybe."

"I'm too old for picture books." He started collapsing his telescope.

"A graphic novel then!"

But Yoshi had already started wandering back toward the Periwinkle Tower.

"I'm sorry, Yoshi!" Tonya called out. "The reason I forgot you can't read is because you're so smart!"

Yoshi squeezed out a smile and kept walking. But digging just wasn't as much fun after that, so we quit earlier than usual.

Mr. Dayberry's Announcement

On Thursday Mr. Dayberry said he had an announcement to make. He sounded so excited that we all actually got quiet. Even Cheerio, the class rat, crept out of his fort to listen—the fort Hunter had made him out of an old baseball cap.

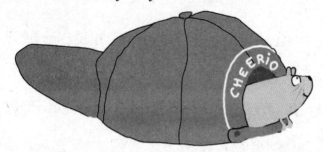

"The Spring Thing is coming up. Does everyone remember the Spring Thing from last year?"

Boris raised his hand. "I wasn't here last spring," he reminded us.

It seemed like Boris had been here forever, but only five or six months ago he had been the new boy.

"Our school has the Spring Thing every year," said Hunter. "There are games and contests."

"And a spelling bee with a prize," I added. "Last year the prize was a pen that wrote in six colors. I wanted it so bad! Sofie won it."

"Now you'll have another chance," said Mr. Dayberry.

"Will there be a bouncy castle again this year?" asked Tonya, adjusting her tiara.

"Yes," said Mr. Dayberry. Then he cleared his throat in that important way. "And this year our class has been invited to take part in the science fair. You'll partner-up, and you and your lab partner will come up with an idea for a science experiment."

"Will there be a prize?" I asked.

"The partners who win will each receive a pair of binoculars."

"I have both a microscope and a telescope already," said Yoshi.

"Who'll judge?" asked Sofie.

"Mayor Kale and Mr. Fogarty will judge."

"This sounds hard," said Hunter.

"Then let's make it fun," said Mr. Dayberry. "Pick something personal for your experiment. Something that means something to you. Something you wonder about."

"Oh, I have an idea! I have an idea!" squealed Tonya. "I have the winning idea," she added, twirling her hair.

"The proof will be in the pudding," said Mr. Dayberry.

Lab Partners

Partnering-up is always scary. You have to move fast, or you'll get left behind.

I had a hard time choosing between Boris and Yoshi. Boris was creative, like me, but harder to boss around.

Yoshi has both a telescope and a microscope already. And even though

he can't read yet, everybody knows he's the smartest. When I thought about how much I would miss him this summer, that settled it. But by the time I got Yoshi's attention, Tonya had already corralled him.

So Boris and I made a beeline for each other. And then Sofie and Hunter, the other two members of the Gum Club, teamed up.

The bell rang. It was Boris's day to carpool. Before I could even start the car, Boris checked the glove compartment. "Anything to eat in here?"

He found half a peanut butter, banana, and popcorn sandwich.

"Don't eat it, Boris! I must have left it in there last Saturday after Hunter's game. It's probably rotten by now!"

As we zoomed home we talked about our experiment. "What should we do?" I asked.

"Mr. Dayberry's already given us

an important clue," said Boris, taking a big bite of the sandwich. "Remember when he said the proof is in the pudding? Let's do a pudding experiment."

"How?" I asked.

"We'll ask Chef Pepper in the school cafeteria to help us make two gigantic barrels of pudding. One barrel will be my favorite flavor, caramel. And the other barrel can be a flavor that means something to you."

"Chocolate!" I shouted. "But Mr. Dayberry said to make our experiment something we've always wondered about."

"Haven't you always wondered what flavor of pudding is the best in the whole world?

"We already know it's either caramel or chocolate. We'll gather scientific data that will answer our question beyond the shadow of a doubt."

I already knew chocolate was the most delicious flavor. But I played along.

"How will we gather the data?"

"Whichever barrel is empty first will confirm that *that* flavor is the best. The proof will be in the pudding that disappears first."

I almost ran off the road. See what I mean about Boris being creative?

Digging with Boris

Friday after school I had to drop Yoshi
off at his new reading tutor's. I gave
Marvin a treat soon as I got home.

Boris came up and we played drums.
I had just begun a drum solo using my
potato masher on Boris's pizza pan
when we heard Tonya's door slam.

Time to quit.

I headed straight down to the tunnel. Sometimes when I got really sad about Yoshi leaving, it helped to dig.

On the brighter side, if there happened to be buried treasure down there, maybe I would find it before anybody else.

Boris joined me after I'd been digging for a while. He brought me a box of chocolate-covered raisins. I was so hungry, I tore into the box and candy flew everywhere.

And then we heard a voice from above.

"I've asked you to be very careful when you eat candy in the tunnel.

Candy attracts ants! But nobody listens."

"We *do* listen, Tonya! It was an accident! We'll pick it up."

"I'm on my way to Scouts," she said. "I can't be here to supervise you, so just make sure to put the trapdoor back in place when you're finished." She headed down the path to the Scout hut.

We dug until it was almost dark. We talked about Yoshi. "What if when Boot Camp is over Uncle Albert decides to take Yoshi back to Japan with him?" My voice got all wavery.

"Don't cry, Mimi. Let's go inside. I'll

make you some rice pudding for dinner." That's when Boris's shovel hit
something weird.

"A dinosaur bone!" he shouted. He
grabbed his chisel. My tears stopped.

It looked like a rounded piece of wood to me. I thought about all the shipwrecks off the coast of Pueblo del Mar. "The top of a treasure chest!"

We both dug like crazy for another half hour. It was pitch black when we set our tools down.

Could this be it?

Boris brushed some dirt away. I felt around for my flashlight and shone it on the tunnel wall.

It was a big fat tree root.

Tonya's Accident

Early the next morning I was dreaming that a tall yellow crane was hoisting a treasure chest out of the ground. A treasure chest that I had discovered in the tunnel. The crane was super loud. *CLICKITY CLACK, CLICKITY CLACK, CLICKITY CLACK...*

And then Marvin leaped up onto the bed and meowed.

I woke up. But the *CLICKITY CLACK*-ing didn't stop. I peeked out the window.

It was Tonya! She was limping toward the street, wheeling her pink suitcase down the bumpy walk. One of her legs was wrapped in a bandage.

"Tonya!" I yelled. "What's going on?" Two more windows flew open below me. We all waited to hear what Tonya would say.

"I'm moving out," she announced. "Nobody listens to me around here."

She pointed toward the big hole. "I *told* you to put the trapdoor back. But you didn't. I fell into the tunnel on my way back from Scouts. And now I'm moving out."

I shoved the window all the way up, grabbed hold of the drainpipe, and slid down. Yoshi and Boris ran out in their pajamas.

We crowded around Tonya and blocked her way.

"Tonya, we're sorry! It got dark and we forgot! Please don't go." I knew Tonya could be bossy. But she belonged with us. Besides, Marvin was absolutely crazy about her.

"Have you had breakfast yet?" asked Boris. "At least have some breakfast before you go. I'll make waffles."

Yoshi grabbed Tonya's suitcase and started wheeling it back up to the front door.

"Okay. But after breakfast I'm moving out."

Once we guided Tonya into Boris's

apartment, I called Sofie and Hunter. They wanted to see Tonya one last time.

Boris set a waffle in front of each of us. He sliced some bananas into a bowl. When I saw the banana slices out of the corner of my eye, they looked just like gold coins.

As Boris passed the maple syrup to Tonya, he asked, "Where will you move?"

"To a new tower where people appreciate me," said Tonya. "To a pink tower. Or a yellow tower maybe. Any tower but the Periwinkle Tower."

"But Tonya," I said. "You made the Gum Club Promise. 'We'll stick together, whatever we do!' Remember?"

"And Tonya," said Yoshi, "don't forget—we're lab partners."

"Yeah," said Hunter. "What about the Wing Ding?"

"You mean the *Spring Thing*," corrected Tonya.

"You love the bouncy castle *so much*," whispered Sofie.

Tonya hesitated. She adjusted her bandage. "Well, I guess I'll stay for the Spring Thing. But after that I'm leaving town."

Tonya Shares, Yoshi Shares

It had been a close call with Tonya that morning. Sometimes trying to keep the Gum Club together was like trying to herd six Marvins.

So that afternoon I invited Tonya up to help me make some slime. I knew she had glitter. I hoped she would bring it with her, so we could make sparkly slime. The moment Tonya limped in, Marvin ran up to her and rubbed his head on her bandage.

"I can't stay long." she said. "I'm allergic to cats." She handed me a big tube of purple glitter.

"Oh, Tonya! Purple's my favorite color!"

"You can keep the tube if there's any left over," she said, stepping around Marvin.

Just as we finished kneading the slime, Yoshi gave the secret knock. He burst in waving an envelope with pretty Japanese stamps on it.

"Look! Uncle Albert
sent me some money!
Would you guys like
to help me spend it?"

"Is it American money or
Japanese money?" asked Tonya.

Yoshi showed us the bill. A twenty!
I pointed to the words "United States
of America" and read them out loud to
Yoshi.

"Who's that guy with the curly
hair?" he asked.

"Jackson," Tonya replied, pointing to his name.

"Andrew Jackson?" asked Yoshi. "Mr. Dayberry said he wasn't very nice to the Indians."

"You mean the Native Americans," corrected Tonya.

"Then let's get rid of him!" I shouted.

Yoshi and I were out the window and down the drainpipe in no time. Tonya took the banister.

Yoshi insisted on hitting the used bookstore first. He bought a couple of *Captain Science* comic books. I settled on *Treasure Island* to read to Marvin. Tonya chose a *Hairdresser* magazine.

We spent the change at the candy store on chocolate-covered raisins.

In the Tunnel with Yoshi

The next day, Sunday, Marvin jumped up onto the reading chair and waited. Every week I have Sunday school with Marvin, right here at home. I hold him in my lap and read out loud to him. He always falls asleep in class.

Today I read to him from his new

book, *Treasure Island*. Soon as he fell asleep I wriggled out from under him and took the drainpipe down to the tunnel. I was getting frustrated. Would I ever find any buried treasure?

The trapdoor was askew. When I looked down, I was caught off guard by two bright reflections. "Hi, Mimi." It was Yoshi—Yoshi's glasses, that is. He was sitting down there all by himself.

"Yoshi! You scared me to death!"

I climbed down and sat across from him.

"I was getting sad again," he said.

"Sad because you're leaving this summer?"

"Yeah. Sometimes it helps to play my ukulele. And I can sing as loud as I want down here. If I could read I wouldn't have to go. It's not fair. Everybody else can read. Why can't I?"

Yoshi played a few chords. Then he

sang "Bury Me Not on the Lone Prairie" in the most mournful voice.

"Yoshi, I have an idea. You can help me study for the spelling bee! And learn to read at the same time."

I was determined to win the spelling bee this time. I had to have that six-color pen. "Come on, let's go. I made some flash cards. Maybe you won't have to go to Boot Camp!"

Yoshi stopped strumming and we both climbed out of the tunnel.

When we got to Tonya's floor, we remembered the trapdoor and ran back outside to replace it.

Yoshi Walks Out

I handed Yoshi my flash cards. Marvin
had been listening to me spell, so I had
chosen words I thought he would like.

"Okay. Spell this," said Yoshi. He
held a flash card up in front of my eyes.

"Tuna. T-U-N-A. Tuna." When Marvin
heard me spell "tuna," he woke up.

"Hmmm. I'm not sure what this word is," said Yoshi, showing me another card.

"Catnip," I said. "C-A-T-N-I-P."

"The next word's really long, so take your time." Yoshi held up the card that said "whisker."

We were getting nowhere. "Come

on, Yoshi! You can't *show* me the word
I'm supposed to spell! That's stupid."

"Then what am I supposed to do? I
can't *read* the words!" Yoshi crumpled
up the flash card and threw it across
the room. Marvin tore after it and
attacked it. Neither of us laughed.

"You called me *stupid*," said Yoshi quietly. For the first time ever, Yoshi walked out of my apartment without saying good-bye.

I was so shocked that no words came out of my mouth.

It Is So. It Is Not.

A minute later I took off down the steps. I banged on Yoshi's door. "Yoshi, open up! I didn't call *you* stupid!"

"What did you say then?" he yelled through the door.

"I said what you *did* was stupid!"

"Same thing!"

"Is NOT!"

"Is SO!"

"Is NOT!"

"Is SO!"

"Is NOT!"

"Is SO!"

"Is NOT!"

"Is SO!"
"Is NOT!"
"Is SO!"
"Is NOT!"
"Is SO!"
"Is NOT!"
"Is SO!"

A door flew open below. Tonya appeared. "PLEASE BE QUIET!" she screamed. Her tiara popped off and hit the stairs.

I dragged myself back up to my apartment. I didn't know what to do. I picked up the pink seashell from China and held it to my ear. But the seashell wasn't talking.

Our Experiments

Monday we were supposed to describe our science fair experiments to the class.

Hunter and Sofie stood up first. "Our experiment is called Rat Race," said Hunter.

Sofie continued: "There's something

I've always wondered about. Does practice *really* make perfect? I practice ballet all the time. And sometimes I can't tell if it makes any difference at all."

"Same here," said Hunter. "Only baseball is my thing."

Sofie reached into Cheerio's cage. She gently picked up the little rat. "Cheerio, our class rat, and Rufus, the rat next door in Ms. Kay's class, will be our assistants. They'll help us find out whether or not practice matters." Sofie kissed Cheerio and set him back in his cage.

"I made a maze out of Legos," said

Hunter. "In the shape of a baseball diamond. We'll carve home plate out of cheese."

We waited to hear what came next. Hunter looked over at Sofie, but she was sound asleep. "Sofie, wake up!"

"I'm sorry," said Sofie. "I had a ballet recital last night and ... Where were we?"

"Spring training," Hunter prompted her.

"Oh yes. So we've started spring training for Cheerio and Rufus every day during lunch. They practice exploring the maze together. But we've been allowing Cheerio twice as much time to practice. He has spring training

without Rufus after school while we clean his cage."

"At the Spring Thing we'll find out whether Cheerio's extra practice helps him find home plate before Rufus does," said Hunter. "Any questions?"

Boris raised his hand. "If Cheerio scores first and eats home plate, will Rufus still get a piece of cheese?"

"Oh yes," Sofie assured him. "There will be plenty of cheese for each rat. And you can have a piece too if you'd like."

Tonya and Yoshi stood up next. Tonya began. "Our experiment is called Is It Hair or Is It Fur? I think about hair a lot. And one thing I've always wondered—and I'm sure you have too—is this: Are hair and fur actually the same thing?"

Yoshi held up his microscope. "We're going to collect hair samples and fur samples, and then examine them using my microscope."

Everyone clapped politely. "Any questions?" Yoshi asked. I raised my hand.

"I found one of Marvin's whiskers on the floor yesterday. I can donate it to science if you'd like, Yoshi."

But Yoshi ignored my question.

"That would be very nice, Mimi," said Tonya.

When it was Boris's and my turn to describe our experiment, my heart wasn't in it. I was so upset about Yoshi ignoring my question that I let Boris do all the talking. He stood up on a stool and described our Proof Is

in the Pudding experiment. Everyone
laughed, including Mr. Dayberry.

Sofie Calls a Meeting

Two days later, on Wednesday after school, Sofie called a meeting of the Gum Club. She was carrying her flashlight. I was sure she wanted us all to work together on our tunnel, and I was eager to start digging.

After we each had cranked a gum

ball out of Boris's machine, we made a huddle and yelled:

"Six members loyal,
six members true.
We'll stick together,
whatever we do!"

But Sofie didn't lead us out to the tunnel. She led us up the spiral staircase to the landing outside my apartment.

She pointed to the door in the ceiling. "Does that lead to the attic?" she asked. "If it does, I wondered if we could fix it up to be my apartment. Then I'll have a place to stay when the tunnel is finished."

"That would be fun!" I said. I climbed to the top of the spiral stairs and pushed the door aside so Sofie could see.

"But you can't stand up in there. The ceiling is too low."

"Maybe I wouldn't *need* to stand," she said, shining her flashlight into the tiny space. "We could make it into a dorm room. I could lie down and sleep up there!"

"There aren't any windows," said Boris. "It's really dark."

"That's okay. I have my flashlight."

Hunter took a peek. "There's an old card table in my basement. Even if there's not room to sit up, maybe you could play cards underneath it. I'll bring it over. That's what they do in dorms. Play cards. And you could sleep under the table, too."

I thought about how much fun it would be playing cards in the reformatory dormatory when I grew up.

"May I take a look?" asked Tonya, bouncing up the stairs.

"Tonya, is your leg better?" asked Sofie. "You're not limping anymore. But you're still wearing your bandage."

"It's better," said Tonya. "I wear the bandage to remind me I'm moving out after the Spring Thing."

"Tonya," Sofie whispered. "You know I don't want you to move out. But if you do, maybe I could have your apartment."

116

Tonya fiddled with her bandage and pretended not to hear.

Yoshi scrambled up last. "If we saw a hole in the roof, I'll set up my telescope and make an observatory. Then we can lie down and star watch in the winter."

The Gum Club took a vote. We all agreed that fixing up Sofie's dorm room was an excellent idea.

Hunter left for baseball practice, and I had treasure on the brain. "Yoshi, would you like to dig with me and Sofie?" I asked.

But Yoshi said he didn't feel like it.

A Sorry Apology

Yoshi had not run up and given the secret knock one time since we had studied for the spelling bee.

At recess we had always played together on the swings. When we got as high up as we could go, we'd let go and see who could jump the farthest.

But the swing beside me had been empty every day this week. On Friday Sofie sat down on the empty swing.

"Mimi, are you sad?" she asked.

"No. Why?" I wound my swing up

as tight as I could and spun around. Maybe Sofie wouldn't see the tear creeping down my cheek.

But it was no use trying to lie to Sofie. So I explained about Yoshi holding the flash cards up in front of my eyes, and how I told him it was a stupid thing to do.

"Oh no," said Sofie.

"But it's been almost a whole week! And he's still mad!" That's when Sofie said something brilliant.

"Did you apologize?"

After the bell rang, Yoshi was out the door and down the steps before I caught up with him.

"Yoshi, wait! Don't you want a ride home?"

"No. I'm walking."

I ran around in front of him and

stopped him. "Yoshi, I have something I'd like to say to you."

Yoshi pushed his glasses up on his nose and looked at me for the first time in five days.

"I'm sorry I said what you did was stupid." Yoshi's face softened. "But you shouldn't show me a flash card when you're asking me to spell a word!"

"So you're sorry or you're *not* sorry?" asked Yoshi.

"I *am* sorry, but it ruins everything if you show me the word I'm trying to spell."

"You don't *sound* sorry,"

Yoshi said as he walked away.

Bringing Out the Pudding

The week before the Spring Thing dragged by. I dug in the tunnel every day after school, and at night I read *Treasure Island* to Marvin before he fell asleep. There were no secret knocks on my door, and I still hadn't found one speck of treasure.

On the morning of the Spring Thing, Boris and I needed help. Chef Pepper had stood by as we multiplied our ingredients by one hundred, and used his humongous mixer. And now there

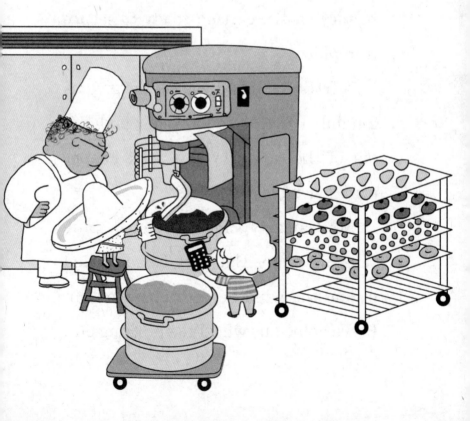

were two big vats of pudding ready to go, one caramel and one chocolate. Chef Pepper handed Boris a giant box of wooden sample spoons.

We found Mr. Bosco out by the bouncy castle, getting ready to secure it in place.

"Mr. Bosco, could you please give us a hand? We need to move our pudding out of the cafeteria and Chef Pepper can't leave his turnovers."

Mr. Fogarty had predicted blue skies for today. But dark clouds rolled in and the wind began to blow as Mr. Bosco helped us wheel the pudding out.

Before the spelling bee began, I saw Yoshi sneak off. He hid under the bleachers. I reached between the benches and waved to him, but he ignored me.

Tonya's tiara popped off when she misspelled "spaghetti."

"It's not fair! I don't even *like* spaghetti!"

The bee wore on. I spelled "bubble" and "kibble."

Later Mr. Dayberry said, "Mimi, please spell 'trouble.'"

"Trouble," I repeated. "T-R-U-B-B-L-E."

Sofie spelled "trouble" correctly, and finally won with the word "ballet." She would go home with the six-color pen for the second year in a row.

Was it right for one person to own two six-color pens? I wasn't so sure.

Tonya Stomps Off

The little kids had to wait until the breeze died down to play inside the bouncy castle. Ms. Marzipan, our music teacher, was prepared. She rounded them up and they had a blast swatting at the big sun-shaped piñata. The school band marched around them playing "Here Comes the Sun." The sky grew darker and darker.

"That piñata may be the only sun we see today," said Mayor Kale. "Mr. Fogarty, couldn't you have helped us out a little with the weather?" Mr. Fogarty laughed. The mayor took his arm. "Shall we begin our rounds?"

Mayor Kale scanned the science fair. She raised her megaphone. "Is everyone ready?"

Then in her normal voice she asked, "Tonya, before we begin, do you have all your equipment set up?"

Tonya nodded.

"Then what's that pretty pink suitcase doing under your table?"

"I'm moving. Right after the Spring
Thing is over."

"Well, I didn't know that. We'll miss
you," said the mayor.

The judges' first official stop was at
the vomiting volcano. At least that's

what Boris called it. One of the big kids had put it together. As she warned the judges to stand back, something caught my eye.

"Mr. Fogarty's tie clip!" I gasped.

"What about it?" asked Boris.

"It's made out of a gold doubloon!"

"I saw that in the lighthouse gift shop," said Sofie.

"Do you think Mr. Fogarty gets a discount on things in the gift shop?" I asked.

"If you're the lighthouse keeper," said Boris, "I bet you can borrow stuff from the gift shop anytime you want."

"If I don't get accepted at the reformatory, I'm taking over Mr. Fogarty's job when he retires,"

I announced. It was starting to look like the only way I would ever get my hands on any treasure would be to borrow it from the gift shop.

Boris was reassuring. "I think you

can count on a free pass to the reformatory after you've worked in the gift
shop a few days. You can have your
cake and eat it too."

Then Sofie whispered, "Mimi? You
know I don't *want* you to move to the
lighthouse. But when you take over Mr.
Fogarty's job, could I have your apartment at the Periwinkle Tower? Then I
could stand up."

We were all nervous. It was our first
science fair. Tonya kept pulling her
long white gloves on and off. Then she
picked up Yoshi's telescope and shoved
it underneath the table.

"We won't be needing this. We'll be using the microscope, not the telescope."

"But it's scientific. And it means something to me!" Yoshi moved the telescope back onto the table.

"But it has nothing to do with hair!" Tonya stowed it back under the table behind her pink suitcase.

When Yoshi set the telescope back on the table, Tonya's tiara popped off. She picked up her white gloves and stormed away.

The Bouncy Castle

The judges found themselves in front of the gigantic Lego maze. Sofie gently lifted Cheerio out of his cage and kissed him. "This is Cheerio, our class rat," she said.

"And this is Rufus, who we borrowed from Ms. Kay's class," said Hunter, cradling the spotted rat in his baseball glove.

The wind blew a bunch of Tonya's hair samples into our pudding vats. Boris had a fit. "I recognize this one," I said, pulling a white strand out of my chocolate pudding. "It's Marvin's whisker!"

I laid the whisker back down on Tonya's black velvet along with the

other hair and fur samples. Boris and I did our best to fish the rest of the hairs out of our pudding.

"And Cheerio beats Rufus by a landslide!"

we heard the mayor announce over her megaphone.

The judges wandered from table to table, listening and taking notes. When they reached our table, Boris handed them each two of the tiny spoons.

"You know I'm a vegetarian," said

the mayor. We assured her that the pudding was safe. The judges took their time tasting.

They peered into both vats and Mayor Kale scribbled something on her clipboard.

Then they moved to the table where

Yoshi was sitting all by himself.

"Well, this looks interesting," said the mayor. "What in the world?"

"Our experiment is called Is It Hair or Is It Fur?" said Yoshi. "Tonya thinks about hair a lot. And one thing she's always wondered—and I'm sure you have too—is this: Are hair and fur actually the same thing? We were able to use my microscope to find out."

"Where *is* Tonya?" asked Mayor Kale. "She hasn't moved away already, has she?"

"I don't know," said Yoshi. "Has anyone seen her?"

"She's upset," said Sofie. "She said she wanted some alone-time in the bouncy castle before all the little kids took over."

Boris asked if he could borrow Mayor Kale's megaphone.

"TONYA!"

Sure enough, she appeared at the window of the castle. She didn't exactly smile, but she gave us one of those royal waves like the queen of England.

Suddenly, there was

a huge gust of wind. All the hair and whiskers blew off the table and the castle itself began bouncing across the

playground. Then the castle rose into the sky, with Tonya inside!

We were speechless.

Mr. Dayberry dialed 911.

Mr. Bosco slapped his forehead.

"I was getting ready to secure the castle when I got interrupted to move pudding!"

The Chase

After we finished being speechless, we screamed. Chef Pepper climbed up into the tower on top of the school and began ringing the bell. Yoshi grabbed his telescope and stood on top of the jungle gym. Everyone swarmed around below him.

We all wanted to know where the castle was headed. We heard sirens. Mr. Dayberry switched his phone to speaker. He held it up, so Yoshi could report what

he saw to Captain Wolfenbarger in her
squad car. "It just bounced off the roof
of the candy store!" shouted Yoshi. More
sirens.

"Now it's floating over Dr. Furr's office!"

"Hold on," said Captain Wolfenbarger. "We're getting reports of a UFO sighting."

"It's not a UFO," Yoshi assured her. "It's a bouncy castle."

Yoshi was quiet for a moment. And then: "It's headed straight for the reformatory!"

I jumped up and down. "That's where *I'll* be in ten years! I wish I were there already so I could welcome Tonya!"

"It just got snagged on the barbed

wire fence," reported Yoshi. "It's losing air! Oh no. Tonya just fell out into the reformatory courtyard."

Sweat ran down Mr. Bosco's face. "Does it look like she's okay?" he asked Yoshi.

"She looks angry."

"Don't worry, Mr. Bosco," said Boris. "She always looks like that."

Tonya's Other Leg

"Uh-oh." Yoshi adjusted his telescope. "Captain Wolfenbarger's car is up on the sidewalk outside the reformatory.... A guard is unlocking the gate.... And now Captain Wolfenbarger is helping Tonya into her car."

With her lights flashing, Captain

Wolfenbarger drove Tonya back to school. She carried Tonya straight into the first-aid tent.

It started to drizzle and then to pour. Almost everyone left. But the five of us Gum Club members huddled together outside the tent to wait for our sixth member to come out. When

Tonya appeared, she had a bandage on her *other* leg.

Then she saw us. And even though it was raining, I could tell she got teary.

We all glommed on to her and gave her the most gigantic hug in the history of the world.

"You all waited for me? In the rain?"

"Of course we waited," said Sofie. "We were worried about you. Don't you remember:

Six members loyal,
six members true...?"

We all shouted the last part together:

"We'll stick together,
whatever we do!"

Tonya smiled.

"Can you walk to my car all right?"

I asked. "I loaded your suitcase into the trunk when it started to sprinkle." I took off my hat. "Here. Put this over your hair."

When we reached the car, I put the top up.

"Where would you like to go?" I asked, holding my breath.

"To the tower."

"Which tower? The pink tower? The yellow tower?"

"Home," she said, "to the Periwinkle Tower."

Boris Hosts a Gum Club Dinner

That evening Boris hosted a special dinner meeting for the Gum Club. Tonya had decided not to move out and we were celebrating. I helped Boris make Tonya's favorite dish.

She smiled when Boris set the tub of ambrosia on the table. He scooped a gigantic serving of the pink and green marshmallow goo onto Tonya's plate.

Hunter opened a bag of peanuts and tossed them to Tonya.

"Peanuts with ambrosia? No, thank you." Then she actually said: "I know I can be bossy sometimes. Thank you all for helping save me, and then waiting for me in the rain."

"We wouldn't have left without you," said Sofie.

"You add a special flavor to the Gum Club," said Boris.

"What kind of special flavor?" Tonya asked.

I was afraid Boris was going to say, "Sour apple," but instead he said, "Kind of a burnt caramel."

Tonya smiled.

I offered Yoshi some chocolate-covered raisins to sprinkle on top of his ambrosia. He took a few, but he still wouldn't look at me.

"Yoshi, did we win first place in the science fair?" Tonya asked.

Yoshi shook his head. "Sorry to let you down."

"That's okay," said Tonya. "And I'm glad you brought your telescope. Otherwise Captain Wolfenbarger never would have been able to find me."

She spread her napkin on her lap. "Who *did* win?"

"The vomiting volcano," said Boris.

"When will people ever learn that science fair volcanos are B-O-R-I-N-G?"

We all laughed. Even Yoshi, who could tell from Boris's disgusted tone of voice exactly what he meant.

The Six-Color Pen

So Tonya was back in the pack. But I was still worried about Yoshi for two reasons.

1. Uncle Albert was coming to get him in a few weeks.
2. He was still ignoring me.

Monday at recess Sofie sat down again on the empty swing beside me. "Hi, Mimi. I brought you something!" She pulled a six-color pen out of her riding boot and offered it to me.

I couldn't believe it. "*Sofie!* Are you *sure?*"

"Sure I'm sure! I have two now, so you should have this one."

I took the pen out of her hand and smelled it. It had that sweet inky smell. I held it to my heart. "Thank you, Sofie. I can't wait until our tunnel is finished."

Sofie pulled a deck of cards out of her other boot and handed them to me. "Would you mind putting these up in my dorm room when you get home?"

Eureka!

Sometimes I get my best brainstorms when I'm brushing Marvin's fur. That's what happened Tuesday after school.

"Eureka!"

Marvin jumped down and ran under the bed.

"If I can't find a treasure chest, I'll pan for gold nuggets! Like they did during the gold rush," I explained to Marvin.

I took the banister down to Boris's apartment and banged on the door.

"What's that smell?" I asked when he flung open the door.

"I'm trying a new pudding recipe. Cotton Candy Caramel. Want to help?"

"I would, but I need to borrow a sifter right away!"

He disappeared into the kitchen. I heard cabinet doors opening and slamming, and things falling out.

Tonya stomped on the floor above.

"Simmer down!" she shouted.

I heard her tiara hit the floor and her window slam shut.

Boris reappeared with a sifter. "Be sure to let me taste whatever it is you're baking," he said.

I spent two solid hours in the tunnel with the sifter and the garden hose, and all I ended up with were two drowned beetles, three bottle caps, and a muddy mess. Not one gold nugget.

Tomorrow I'd go back to digging with a shovel.

Mr. Bosco

Yoshi continued to go out of his way to avoid me. On Thursday it rained during recess. I cornered Yoshi and asked him if he'd like to jump on the trampoline in the gym with me. He said he didn't feel like it.

When I got home from school I heard

a whooshing sound. I slogged up the steps to my apartment, but Mr. Bosco's vacuum cleaner blocked my way.

"Watch yourself, Mimi!"

"Hi, Mr. Bosco!"

I heard Marvin meow, so I stepped over the hose and skipped on up.

Mr. Bosco turned off the vacuum. "Mimi? There's something I've been meaning to ask you. Usually I have to replace the carpet between your and Yoshi's apartments every few months. You two wear it out in no time. But it looks brand-new. I've barely had to vacuum it. Are you and Yoshi still friends?"

"I did something that hurt Yoshi's feelings. And I apologized. And tried to explain why I did it! But he still doesn't want to play with me."

"What if you just apologized for hurting his feelings and left off the explanation?"

I slumped. That seemed harder somehow.

"Let's practice. Pretend I'm Yoshi." Mr. Bosco put on his glasses.

I took a deep breath. "Hi, Yoshi. I'm sorry I hurt your feelings. But you shouldn't have shown me the flash cards!"

Mr. Bosco
put up his
hand and shook
his head. "Try again.
No 'buts' this time."

I sighed. "Hi, Yoshi. I'm sorry
I hurt your feelings, but . . ."

"Try again," said Mr. Bosco.

"But it's harder that way!"

"Six little words are all you need to
say," said Mr. Bosco. He set down the

vacuum and counted off the words on his fingers:

"I'm sorry I hurt your feelings."

Marvin gave *another* MEOW. This one was as loud as Captain Wolfenbarger's siren. Mr. Bosco wished me good luck and started whooshing again.

Soon as I burst into my apartment, Marvin ran to the refrigerator. He stared up at the door handle.

I gave him a tiny piece of cheese. I grabbed my flashlight. Marvin blocked my way. I knelt down to pet him, but Marvin bounded back to the refrigerator.

"I know you want more cheese, Marvin. And I know you want me to read to you. But I've just *got* to dig for treasure before it gets dark."

He gave a brokenhearted meow.

"I'm sorry I hurt your feelings," I said to Marvin.

It took me a minute to realize that I had done it!

I picked up the pink seashell from China. "I'm sorry I hurt your feelings," I said to the shell.

I held the seashell to my ear, but all I could hear was Mr. Bosco's vacuum cleaner.

Treasure

"I'll be back at dinnertime," I promised Marvin. I was out the window and down the drainpipe.

Tonya came out to supervise me. A few minutes later Boris lowered a bucket of banana pudding into the tunnel along with a bundle of spoons.

"Boris, why is there a toothbrush sticking out of your back pocket?" asked Tonya.

"In case I find a dinosaur bone! It's what scientists use to clean fossils."

When it started getting dark, both Boris and Tonya left.

"I'm sorry I hurt your feelings!" I muttered every time my shovel hit a rock. "I'm sorry I hurt your feelings!"

When it got too dark to see, I stopped digging. I threw the shovel over my shoulder. It clanked against the wall behind me. CLANKED. It did not thud. This was not another tree root.

I picked up the shovel and poked at the wall. I tried to dig out a few roots that had grown around the thing. I gave up and clawed some dirt away with my fingers.

Could it be? It was hard to tell, but I thought I felt the side of a box— and then I felt a hinge.

The upside-down pudding bucket made a good place to prop up my flashlight. I grabbed the pickax and laid into the wall around the treasure chest. The ground would not give. I popped a few rocks out and chopped for another forty-five minutes. It was long past dinnertime, but the box was almost free.

I tugged with all my might. The chest came loose. On the next try I wrestled it out and fell backward. As the chest hit the ground beside me, I heard the coins inside clink!

I shone my flashlight on the box. I tried to open the lid, but there was a latch that wouldn't even begin to budge.

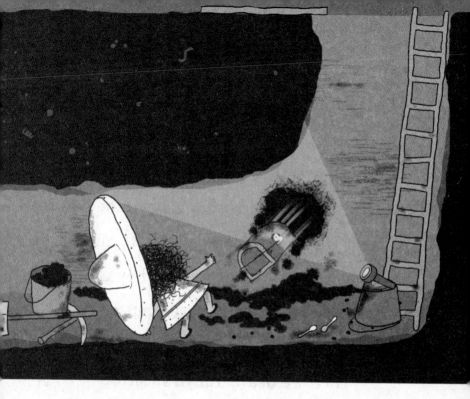

I got a little carried away and did a
victory dance, swinging the flashlight
in my hand like a big searchlight.

"Hey, Mimi!" It was Boris, at his
window. "What's going on out there?"

"I found buried treasure!"

In no time at all Boris was down in the tunnel beside me. An instant later I was a little surprised to see Yoshi's red sneakers scrambling down the ladder. He was moving so fast, he almost ended up on top of Boris. They examined the box with big eyes, but neither of them could open it.

Then we heard Tonya's voice.

"I found a treasure chest, Tonya!"

It was the first time ever that Tonya didn't have a quick reply. I shone the flashlight up to make sure she was okay. Her eyes were about to pop out, and her mouth was gaping.

Then she got her voice back.

"Open it!"

We tried every single tool, but the latch did not budge.

Boris must have phoned Hunter, and Hunter must have phoned Sofie, because they popped up right behind Tonya. Sofie was in her nightgown.

"We should take it inside so it's safe," I said.

"I can borrow Buster's lock-picking kit tomorrow," said Hunter. "I'm sure it will work."

"Who's Buster?" asked Boris.

"My big brother."

"I didn't know you had a brother," said Tonya.

"He doesn't live at home. He's studying at the reformatory," said Hunter.

The Buried Treasure Rule

The treasure chest was only a little bigger than Marvin's carrier, but it weighed a ton. The handle had rusted flat against the top.

I scooted the box to Boris, and he and Yoshi heaved it up beside Tonya. "I'm so glad I didn't move away!" she said.

"We can keep it in my apartment until we bust it open," said Boris, as he and Hunter carried it through the front door.

"No, Boris," said Tonya, who was now back to her normal burnt-caramel self. "You're right above the lobby. It would be too easy for a burglar to steal the treasure. We'll carry it on up to my apartment."

Boris and Hunter lugged it up a floor.

"My apartment is even safer," volunteered Yoshi.

Hunter and Boris took a break. Yoshi and Sofie hauled it up another flight of steps to the landing outside Yoshi's apartment.

As Yoshi unlocked his door I heard my own voice say,

"It's my treasure. And I'm keeping it in my apartment."

Everyone paused. No one said anything for a minute.

"Aren't we going to share the treasure?" Boris finally asked.

"Well, I think the rule is that buried treasure belongs to the finder," I said. "And I found the treasure."

Five mouths hung open. Five legs swung over the banister ready to slide back down.

"Could somebody please help me carry it up to my apartment?" I asked.

"I have to go put the trapdoor back in place," said Tonya.

"I'll help you, Tonya," said Yoshi.

He and Tonya slid down the banister behind Sofie and Hunter.

Boris helped me carry the treasure up, but he didn't stick around. He gave Marvin a scratch behind the ears, said, "Good night, Marvin," and left.

A few weeks ago, Yoshi walked out without saying good-bye, and tonight Boris did the same. I ran to the window. I wanted to say good-bye to *somebody*. "Good night, Tonya!" I yelled. But the trapdoor was already back in place, and Tonya had disappeared.

For an instant I got a sinking feeling about my friends. But then I saw the treasure chest sitting beside my reading chair, safe in my apartment. When you have a treasure chest, maybe it's okay not to have friends.

Under My Hat

Friday at lunch, no one said much to me. I *knew* something was wrong when I offered Boris half of my peanut-butter-chocolate-chip sandwich and he shook his head no.

It was Yoshi's day to carpool. After school I saw him climb onto the bus. I remembered how he used to sing "Every little thing gonna be all right." Would he ever ride with me again?

"Hunter, want me to drive you to the baseball field?" I asked as he walked up to my car.

"No. I have rat duty this week. But I promised to let you borrow this, so here it is."

He pulled a black case out of his backpack and unfolded it. Inside were dozens of shiny tools all lined up. Some looked like the tools Dr. Molar used to clean my teeth. "It's my brother

Buster's lock-picking kit. He said to keep it under your hat."

I lifted my hat and stuck the case underneath it.

"Oh, wait." He handed me a tiny can of oil. "Buster said to squeeze two drops into the latch. Let it soak in, and then the tools will work like a charm."

It felt funny riding home by myself. But the minute I burst into my apartment—even before I gave Marvin a treat—I squeezed two drops of Buster's oil into the latch on the treasure chest.

I offered Marvin a tiny piece of cheese. I still didn't feel right. Marvin jumped up on my lap and I began brushing his fur. That's when I had another brainstorm. Parties always seemed to help. I'd have an opening party tomorrow!

I picked up my six-color pen and

made five invitations. I used one color
for each of the six lines, only this time
I didn't feel like adding dots.

You're invited to the Grand Opening
of the TREASURE CHEST
Tomorrow, Saturday, at 1:00, in Apt. 4

RSVP   Your friend, MiMi

P.S. Both Chocolate Pudding
and Caramel Pudding will be served.

Five RSVPs

After I delivered the invitations, I climbed down into the tunnel to dig. Nobody else showed up. If I found *more* treasure, maybe I would have enough to share.

When I was too hungry to dig anymore I climbed out, put the trapdoor back, and decided to make mashed potatoes for dinner.

Soon as I opened the door I smelled perfume. Five RSVPs had been slipped under my door!

Two were in Tonya's pink envelopes. I picked up one of them. It said "From Yoshi"! He must have asked Tonya to read the invitation to him. And then she must have helped him reply.

I can't come.
I am meeting
with my reading
tutor. ~Yoshi

I opened the other pink envelope.

Did you mean 1 p.m. or
1 a.m.? If you meant
1 p.m., I'll be washing
my hair. If you meant
1 a.m., I'll be asleep.
                    —Tonya

And then I read Hunter's RSVP.

I have baseball
practice. I can't come.
Please return Buster's
lock-picking kit after
your party. —Hunter

Then Boris's.

I'll be working on a new pudding recipe. I won't be able to make it to your Grand Opening. -Boris

Maybe Sofie could come! I tore open her RSVP.

I'm sorry I can't come. I'm going to a horse show. -Sofie

Nobody could come to my party. Nobody wanted to carpool. Nobody seemed interested in digging in the tunnel anymore. And Yoshi hadn't given the secret knock in weeks. I might as well have been kicked out of the Gum Club.

That's when it hit me. Nobody wanted to be my friend anymore.

I started to cry.

My Former Friends

I thought about Yoshi and how much I would miss him this summer. How much I *already* missed him.

I thought about Tonya and how much Marvin loved her. How relieved I was when she decided not to move away. How she let me keep the purple glitter.

I thought about Boris. How much fun it had been playing drums and planning new recipes with him.

I thought about Sofie. How amazing it felt when she gave me the six-color pen. For no reason.

I thought about how funny Hunter was—thinking the pink seashell spoke in Chinese.

I thought about how happy I was back when the pink seashell was talking.

I picked it up and held it to my ear. Maybe this time it would tell me what to do. But the shell was still silent.

and

Emergency Gum Club Meeting

I stood in the middle of the room for so long that Marvin clomped down from the windowsill and wandered over. He looked up at me and wailed the longest *MEOWWWWWW* I had ever heard.

Then I knew what to do. I opened my window, stuck my head out, and gave the emergency whistle.

Within minutes everyone was in my apartment, including Sofie and Hunter. They all knew that the emergency whistle meant "urgent," no matter what.

We all mumbled the Gum Club Promise. But when we got to the part "We'll stick together, whatever we do," no one looked at me.

"I called this meeting of the Gum Club because I think we should share the treasure," I said. "And I think we should open the treasure chest right now. Even though I haven't had a chance to make any pudding."

209

"And, Yoshi." I took a deep breath and looked him in the eyes. I repeated the six words that Mr. Bosco had taught me:

"I'm sorry I hurt your feelings."

Five blank faces lit up. Make that six. Because even though I had decided not to keep all the treasure for myself, I couldn't believe how happy I felt.

The Big Bust

I reached under my hat and removed Buster's lock-picking kit. I pulled out the first tool.

No luck. I tried another tool. Finally, when each of us had tried every tool, I asked, "Can Buster come over tonight?"

"No," said Hunter. "He can't."

"When *can* he come over?"

Hunter's face turned red. "Not for a few more months."

He took the drainpipe down and was back in a flash with the pickax from the tunnel. "Mimi, would you like to go first?" he asked.

I swung the pickax as hard as I could. When it hit the box, it made the most beautiful sound. The gold doubloons jingled, and the jewelry rattled.

Marvin ran under the bed. But the chest didn't open.

I handed the pickax back to Hunter.

On his very first try the box splintered
and shattered.

Rusty nuts and bolts flew all over
the apartment. A wrench shot through
the air and almost broke the window.

Nobody said anything for the longest

time. There were funny old screw-drivers and folding wooden measuring sticks. There were wrenches and awls and a hand drill. A dirty hammer.

Boris picked up something that looked like a petrified ham sandwich.

It was wrapped in moldy paper.

Tonya broke the silence. "Boris! Please don't eat it!"

Boris looked at her like she was crazy. Then everybody burst out laughing. Everybody except me. I started to cry. Again.

"It's an old tool chest!" giggled Sofie. Then she noticed my tears. She came over and touched my arm. "Mimi, why are you crying?" She waited for me to answer.

The Pink Seashell Pipes Up

But I couldn't talk. Soon everybody came over and huddled around me. They gave me a five-person hug.

"Mimi, please don't cry," said Yoshi softly.

Then I really broke down. Yoshi was talking to me!

"This is crazy!" I sobbed. "Why are you all being so nice to me?"

"Because you wanted to share the treasure with us!" said Sofie, smoothing my hair.

"But there isn't any treasure!"

Tonya rolled her eyes. She handed me a tissue. I blew my nose.

Yoshi said, "Mimi, don't you remember Nobody's birthday party?"

"What about it?"

"We all shared presents with one another. It was so much fun!"

"And it didn't matter what the presents were," said Sofie. "Yoshi gave me a rock!"

"It was a special rock!" insisted Yoshi.

This time we all laughed. We couldn't stop.

"Wait a sec," said Hunter. He picked up the pink seashell from the mantel and held it to his ear. His eyes almost popped out. "Mimi! Listen!" He presented the shell to me on his baseball glove.

I held it to my ear. The shell was laughing. It must have heard everything we said.

Everyone crowded around me again to listen to the shell. Before I passed it to Yoshi, I changed ears and I swear the shell said,

You have something more precious than gold.

At first I thought the shell needed glasses. I dropped down on my hands and knees and looked under the bed just to make sure I hadn't overlooked a diamond or an emerald.

Then I stood up. I saw Yoshi and all the rest of the Gum Club members staring back at me with shining eyes.

"Well," I said. "I guess being back with the Gum Club ain't too shabby."

"*Isn't* too shabby," said Tonya.

A Surprise

Monday morning Mr. Dayberry told us Hunter had an announcement to make.

Hunter stood up. "Remember when I made a fort for Cheerio out of my old baseball cap? Today I found six babies in the fort!"

We all gasped. Quietly we made a line and tiptoed up to take a peek. They didn't look like rats. None of them had any fur. They were pink. One had three big dots on its skin. The dots made me laugh.

"Whose babies are they?" I asked. We all knew Cheerio was a boy.

"We must have been mistaken about Cheerio's gender," said Mr. Dayberry.

"Who's the dad then?" asked Tonya. "There has to be a dad."

"Maybe Cheerio and Rufus got married during spring training," said Sofie.

Normal

Things were finally shifting back to normal. I never realized how terrific just plain *normal* could be.

Hunter told me that because I liked dots, he was going to name the spotted baby rat after me. "Only since she has *three* dots, I'm naming her Mi-mi-mi."

Yesterday somebody, probably Boris, left a box of chocolate-covered raisins in my mailbox.

And Sofie asked me to go horseback riding! Since I've never ridden a horse before, she said we'd ride double. She would sit behind me to make sure I didn't fall off.

Tonya slid a note under my door. Even though it smelled good, at first I was afraid to read it.

Dear Mimi,
Thank you for sharing the treasure. Even though there wasn't any treasure.
♡ Tonya

Loose Ends

The Big Dig will continue. For now,
Sofie's dorm room has a card table with
a deck of cards and a pillow. So even
though she still can't sneak over every
night, at least she can climb up there
on Wednesday afternoons and play soli-
taire by flashlight underneath the table.

And despite the fact that he'll bring us a suitcase full of presents, none of us wants to think about Uncle Albert coming. He hasn't changed his mind about taking Yoshi away to Reading Boot Camp. For the whole summer.

But until that day, Yoshi's back to carpooling with me and belting out "Every little thing gonna be all right" at the top of his lungs.

You know how I hate being wrong.

But the shell was right.

Even with no treasure chest in the picture, having my friends back makes me feel like a million bucks.

No, make that a million gold doubloons.